second helpings

second helpings

New tales featuring character favorites

dara girard

contents

books by dara girard

Duvall Sisters

The Glass Slipper Project

Taming Mariella

A Reluctant Hero

Kayode Sisters

The Language of Flowers

Sooner or Later

This Time Forever

Henson Series

Table for Two

Gaining Interest

Careless Rapture

Dangerous Curves

Familiar Stranger

Clifton Sisters

The Sapphire Pendant

The Amber Stone

The Emerald Ring

Novels

Dream of Me

Honest Betrayal

The Daughters of Winston Barnett

Winterwood Lane

Piece of Cake

This Changes Everything

Collections

Domestic Disturbance (written as Dara Benton)

The Lady Next Door and Other Stories

Holiday Hearts

School Days: Five Story Collection

Lost and Found

Five Holiday Tales

10 Holiday Stories

When the Snow Falls

The Blue Mango Collection

introduction

Dear Reader,

Sometimes you just want to go back.

Many times when I end a novel, I am ready to jump into the next project without thinking about the one I've just finished.

But sometimes there are characters who ask for new stories. These story requests don't always come right away. Many times it will be years later and a character will say, "Guess what I have to tell you," and off the story goes.

Here are a few bonus stories (related to some of my series) that I've written over the years. At the beginning of each tale I've included some thoughts on how the story came into being.

Hope you enjoy.

Dara Girard

one wish

. . .

In "The Glass Slipper Project", Gabriella and Tony's story gets overshadowed by the main couple, but I enjoyed them so much I wanted to revisit them. So I decided to write a bonus story from Tony's point of view.

A wounded soldier who felt past him prime and who also had feelings for his boss's fiancee was a story ripe for telling. Since everything ends well in the novel, with a number of twists and turns, I thought I'd give him a chance to be the hero he deserved to be.

A LIVE WIRE.

A venomous snake.

A deadly inferno.

Tony Blake knew the danger was real but couldn't resist the pull. He bit his lip as he sat in his car facing his next mission. That's what he'd started calling them. Not assignments—missions. And each one was getting harder. He stared up at the stylish hotel as clouds drifted low overhead, their slightly grayish tinge hinting at the possibility of rain or perhaps they reflected his mood. He felt as if he were living under his own personal storm cloud.

He briefly closed his eyes before he stared at the building again. He was supposed to meet her here—his torment, his angel— and he was already late. He could see her sitting by the window in the lobby waiting for him.

Gabriella Duvall. His boss's fiancée. For the past several weeks Tony had been Alex's stand-in. Alex was too busy to deal with what he considered 'trifles' such as selecting the different catering companies for the wedding party or taking his future wife out to buy paintings and other furnishings for their new home.

That was what Tony was for. Alex paid him well to make his life run smoothly and handling a fiancée Alex didn't have time for, was one of those tasks. At first Tony didn't mind. He had gotten used to being Alex's good manners, but this assignment—no mission—was getting difficult. He never thought he'd feel like this. Of all the four Duvall sisters Alex had to choose, why did it have to be Gabby?

He could have resisted the eldest sister, Mariella, that woman couldn't pass by a reflection without looking at herself; the second sister, Isabella, didn't have her sisters' beauty but she was kind and smart, no problem there and the last sister, Daniella, was sweet but way too young for him to notice. But Gabby. If only she was young enough, but she wasn't. She was all woman to him and it was the first thing he'd seen when he first met her. Those doe eyes; that black hair she kept in a long braid; that gorgeous full figure. A man could get happily lost in those curves and never be found.

He'd been attracted, but he hadn't thought much of it at first. She was a gorgeous woman, but then…he started to get to know her more and he liked her mind, he liked her smile. He liked *her*.

No…he wanted her and that wasn't possible. She was getting married to his boss.

His cell phone rang. Tony glanced at the number and knew it was her, but didn't answer.

He swallowed and drummed his fingers on the steering wheel. He had to go inside. She would be waiting for him. He wasn't being paid to keep her waiting. If she called Alex and complained about him that would cause more trouble than he needed. He was here to participate in a wine and chocolate pairing event with her. It had been a suggestion from the wedding planner as something the guests might enjoy. Gabby wanted to try it first before committing to it. Alex had a last minute meeting he wanted to go to so Tony was his stand-in. Again. At least he hadn't been stupid enough to offer to pick her up. He needed to keep as much distance between them as he could manage. The Wine Lovers and Advocates hosted event was almost a forty minute drive away from the picturesque town of Hydale in upstate New York where she lived.

Tony sent her a quick text telling her he'd be there soon then checked his reflection in the rearview mirror and smoothed down his stripped tie.

Today would be the last time he did this. It had to be. He had to tell her he couldn't see her anymore because…because he was busy. He'd make up some lie that would sound convincing. He'd tell Alex too. Either that or he could really scare her by telling her the truth and confessing how he felt about her. That would get her running.

And the shock and possible disgust on her face would hurt, but he already knew heartbreak was in store for him. Because no matter what happened, how she responded, it wouldn't change how he felt. He'd still want her. He knew she was marrying Alex to save her family. He found that admirable and Alex made it clear that he only wanted a pretty wife with connections, so it wasn't a love match. But Tony knew he was no replacement, even though he wanted Gabby to know that she was worthy of love. That someone did love her.

But he knew that didn't matter. He was no prize. The Duvall sisters barely noticed him. And he didn't have a chance with a woman like Gabby. Who would want an ordinary man like him? Tony glanced down at his leg—a leg that was still attached, but would never be the same—and softly swore. He'd always walk with a limp. He'd always be seen as a wounded soldier to those who knew his past; a crippled guy with graying hair for those who didn't.

He wasn't a hero. Just a man who still panicked at the sound of firecrackers on the Fourth of July. A man who ducked when a car backfired. He should be over it. He'd gotten better. But not enough. The Army had given him stability, freeing him from a childhood baked in chaos. He'd survived his mother and a stepfather, both too broken by life to give him any guidance. His birth father had been a brief moment of calm; he didn't remember much but did recall the scent of his blue wool sweater and a feeling of peace, but after his passing when Tony was five the peace ended. His mother tried to reclaim that peace with a series of relationships that never ended well and a bitterness that continued to grow until her heart stopped when he was nineteen.

But by that time he had a new family and purpose—the Army. It had given him a reason to live. To exist. People noticed him. He had a place in life. Order. Then after the battlefield, chaos seemed to reign again. Civilian life was like a foreign city with a different language and culture. He had a hard time adjusting.

He wore his father's wool sweater, which he'd kept, all the time, even in the summer, sweating like a hog and looking crazy, but not caring. He'd been briefly homeless, though never on the streets. He managed to live on different couches and find shelter in basements for days and weeks, enough people pitying him so that the streets didn't become a permanent home although the possibility had been there.

And through it all he kept his father's sweater. It was his shield, his shelter. He felt his father's presence and it kept him through the transition as he listened to the kind but empty words of counselors. But he'd gotten a life again. Because of Alex Carlton. Alex had turned his life around. Alex had allowed him to see the world in a new way and he was never hungry, never worried where his next meal would come from or where he could stay. He had a steady job, a job he liked. A boss he liked. He couldn't risk it. Alex was more than a boss and a friend he was an anchor.

And without an anchor he was lost.

Chaos always called to him. It was always within reach.

Alex kept him safe.

But Gabby was danger.

Not only because of his attraction to her, but because she encouraged him to dream. To hope again of a life he'd let die as a child. To become the man his father had been. To be a husband and father himself. He'd stopped dreaming that years ago.

And he hadn't missed it. Until now. Now it was like the faint scent of cut apple slices lingering in a fruit bowl. For years he felt aged, as if everyone else around him were more carefree, while his limp seemed to remind him he had one foot in the grave. With Gabby he felt less ancient, more alive—free. Free from everything that had once been a burden to him—his past, his fears. With her he forgot about the limp, the years between them. All that he lacked.

But it was foolish to think—even image—such beauty could be his. She was being nice because she was kind. He'd gotten a taste of heaven and had become greedy. But no more.

He didn't know what he'd do after the wedding when he'd have to see Alex and Gabby together all the time. How would he manage his feelings? Could he temper them enough when they were already running rampant? They captured his mind, holding him hostage, filling his dreams, torturing his thoughts. Tony took a deep, steadying breath and stepped out of his car. His skin felt hot despite the spring breeze.

This was a new battle and he had to fight. He had to win.

At all cost.

"You didn't talk much," Gabby said as they exited the hotel. "Are you feeling all right?"

The scent of rain hung in the air from a light drizzle that had dampened the grass and sidewalk but the clouds had drifted from the sky leaving it a clear blue.

"I'm fine," Tony said. He would only walk her to her car and then he'd be free. He'd managed to survive nearly an hour and a half sampling different wines and possible chocolate pairings. He'd never done something like that before and he remembered mentioning that to her. Gabby then had him taste a chocolate brownie with an Italian pinot grigio. He hadn't expected much, but then when he took a bite before sipping the wine a burst of fruitiness, once hidden, came forth in a surprising way. He remembered staring at her amazed.

A sly grin touched her lips. "It's not the first time I've done something like this," she'd told him. "I only said I wanted to do this again because I wanted Alex to pay for it. Does that make me bad?"

Tony took another sip. "I won't tell him."

"It will be our little secret."

"Hmm."

He glanced up at the now clear sky remembering that moment. He had plenty of secrets. He hadn't told her how he felt or that he couldn't see her again. He'd tell her that later. Right now he needed to send her safely on her way. Mission accomplished.

She stopped walking. "What's wrong?"

Tony looked at her car in a mild panic. It was only a few yards away. He nudged her forward. He had to keep her walking. "Nothing. I had a good time." He smiled hoping that would convince her.

"One day we should try a bunch of chocolate and wine pairings. It doesn't have to be anything fancy. We could break up regular chocolate bars and try different arrangements."

"Hmm."

She touched his sleeve. "I had a wonderful time, thanks to you."

He winced when her hand brushed his sending an electric current of desire through him. "It was nothing."

"Are you hurting?"

All over. He stopped in front of her car. "Drive safe."

She didn't move. She looked at him. A look that hurt: The look of pity. She might as well hand him a cane and start calling him "Gramps." But the look was good. It forced him to face reality; it allowed his dream to die. She didn't see him as a man and she never would.

"Do you mind if we walk a little? The hotel has a nice courtyard," she said. "After all that chocolate and wine I could use the exercise."

He stared at her. Her words were like an arrow popping a balloon; bright sunshine breaking up a storm cloud. He blinked and realized the look of pity had been his imagination. Right now she looked curious, a little concerned but there was no pity there and she seemed to want to spend time with him. Or was that his imagination too?

"Unless… you have something else you need to do," she added hesitant.

Tony shoved his hands in his pockets. He tightened his hand around his car key. He should send her away. He should say no. He should blame his leg. He should turn and walk away. He needed to. He had to.

He swallowed. He wouldn't. Not yet. He'd endure this sweet torture for a few minutes more. "No, I'm not busy."

***

She was only doing the sensible thing Gabby thought as she walked beside Tony along the red brick pathway in the courtyard, listening to the high pitched chirp of a bird singing in the distance. Spring had been kind so far this year. It was perfect wedding weather.

And she needed all the help she could get if she wanted this wedding to happen without incident. Therefore making sure she looked her best today made perfect sense. It didn't matter that it was only for her fiancé's assistant, and, true, she didn't *really* need to wear the new silk blouse and diamond earrings Alex had bought her. But since her parents' passing and the current financial hardship that had forced her to adjust and restyle what clothes she could find so that she didn't look shabby, she now took every opportunity she could to dress her best and show off her new outfits.

It all made perfect sense. Shouldn't she look her best no matter whom she was with? She was a Duvall after all and appearances always mattered. Her mother had taught her that.

Of course, at times, she did care a little too much about how Tony saw her, but as Alex's assistant it was important he liked her too, right? It was sensible to be aware of his opinion as well since he could influence his boss.

Gabby stole a glance at Tony, the sun's rays seeming to polish his brown skin, casting shadows along the hard edge of his jaw as he stared at something ahead. She was glad he wasn't looking at her because sometimes… sometimes the way he looked at her—the way he made her feel—didn't feel sensible at all. Words left her. Her breath caught. But it was probably because of nerves. She was getting close to her wedding day and there was so much pressure to make sure everything was perfect. She couldn't disappoint anyone. Her sisters depended on her.

She was the sensible one.

Marrying Alex Carlton was sensible. Saving her family home was sensible. Having feelings for a man nearly twice her age with no wealth of his own was crazy.

She was smart. Not brilliant, but practical with enough insight to see a situation and make an accurate assessment. She had no use for romance. Especially now. What was romance when the bills were stacked high and the fridge lay bare? Alex had already shown her the future in store for her when she married him. He had already gifted her with gorgeous jewelry and expensive designer clothes.

And yet…

She cast another glance at Tony. He'd been quiet most of today and that wasn't like him. She liked his company because he was easy to talk to and she found him interesting. She had suggested the walk in the courtyard hoping he'd feel more at ease, instead of how he had acted inside the luxury hotel where the event had been held. But he was still silent and withdrawn.

Perhaps he'd been bored. Perhaps the event hadn't interested him as much as it had her. She knew the feeling. Was it strange to find one's future spouse boring? Alex was a little aloof in temperament, but Gabby didn't need much affection. She had plenty from her three sisters.

Alex was pleasant enough. Suitable. She'd known him as a child and he was nothing like the boy who'd once stolen her bicycle. They got on well. But Tony.

Gabby closed her eyes, missing the rock in her path that caused her to stumble forward. Tony quickly caught her, briefly enveloping her in a spicy woodsy fragrance that made her skin tingle. He released her just as quickly. "Are you okay?"

"I'm fine, sorry. I should be paying more attention."

His dark gaze assessed her before he turned away.

A strange little flutter entered her chest, surprising her. Her deceitful heart had been doing that strange dance more and more over the past few weeks and with deeper impact. It only happened around him; when she thought of him; when she saw him. She liked how he smiled. How he listened. Even how he walked, the limp didn't bother her. It made him who he was. And she wondered…

"If you had one wish what would it be?" she said then covered her mouth. She hadn't meant to ask him that, it wasn't a sensible question, but the words left her mouth before she could stop them. Perhaps it was the wine talking.

He turned to her surprised. "Wish?"

She nodded, her face burning with embarrassment but curiosity kept her going. "Yes, just one."

Tony shook his head. "I don't know." He bit his lip then said in a low voice, "How about you?"

"I wish you had met me before this."

"Before what?"

She waved her hand, her engagement ring sparkling in the sunlight. "Before my family lost its fortune."

He fell quiet a moment then said, "Why?"

"Because then you might see me differently." Tears touched her eyes but she couldn't pinpoint the root of her sadness. Was it regret? Disappointment? Shame? The Duvall women were known for their pride but life had trampled on most of it. Others had suffered worse. But if Tony had met her before, he wouldn't have had to stand up for her against the haughty and impossibly slender Elaine Tremain at the party months ago. Elaine had always been catty but now felt bolder with her insults and had taken the opportunity at the Montpelier Mansion to make fun of Gabby's healthy appetite, generous figure and lack of funds, but Tony had come to her aid and complimented her in a way that still made her blush.

She was used to men finding her attractive. She was used to men flirting with her. But Tony did something no man had ever done before. He made her feel a kinship. A connection she'd never felt with anyone outside of her family. She'd had crushes and infatuations but this feeling was something she couldn't yet identify.

Since that moment at the party she'd had a strange urge to feed him because he seemed like a man who could use a little tender care. Working for Alex couldn't be easy and sometimes she saw a look of hunger on his face. The expression was always fleeting and didn't make sense because he was solidly built and looked far from weak. But despite his kind mouth, gentle eyes and calm, steady presence there was something hollow about his features. Something missing—a hunger.

For what she wasn't quite sure, but food had always been her comfort and she hoped it could comfort him too. It was one of the reasons why she'd been happy to go to the chocolate and wine pairing event with him. Watching the brief moments of pleasure on his face while he sipped the wine or tasted the chocolate, especially the brownie and pinot grigio, gave her a private thrill. But the moment hadn't lasted as long as she'd hoped. "You must think me very mercenary to marry a man for money."

He shook his head again, his voice soft and tender. "You know I don't think that."

Gabby sighed, glad he was talking; glad the distance

that had been seeping between them was fading away. "When my parents were alive the Duvalls were the envy of the town. Our futures seemed to shine the brightest and now we're hardly a shadow of ourselves. I want to see us shine again."

"You don't have to explain anything to me."

"I do. I want…I want you to understand."

He squinted up at the sky, his jaw twitched. "I do understand."

"But you're angry with me."

He paused then looked at her. "I'm not angry."

"I can hear it in your voice and see it in your eyes."

His expression darkened, his eyes capturing hers. "No," he said his deep tone holding a fierceness she'd never heard before. "You don't know what you see. And if I had one wish it would be that you understood me… completely."

She didn't understand his words or ask him to explain them. Instead they continued their walk in silence until he suggested they turn back, and Gabby could think of no reason to stay.

One wish.

He'd missed his chance. He could have told her how he felt and then…and then she wouldn't want to be around him anymore. She wouldn't worry about what he thought of her. Tony drove home barely noticing the sky brilliant with color as the sun set. All he could think about was the surprise on Gabby's face, the hurt he'd sensed in her voice thinking he'd been angry with her. Why would she even think that?

Anger had once been a problem of his. His past two relationships had ended badly. All the blame was his. The war hadn't changed him. Anger had. Anger had lingered inside of him before the war and grown even worse after. He had fought for his country, but a feeling of triumph didn't last. No one taught him how to live on past victories, quiet moments, times without a mission. Old war stories grew stale; nobody really cared about him for long.

He swore. She was right. She had read him. He *had* been angry. But not at her. Never at her. Again the blame was all his.

When he saw Gabby again at her engagement party the anger welled up in him again. He thought he'd be able to handle his warring emotions but he'd lied to himself. He left the party unable to endure it anymore. He'd told Alex he wasn't feeling well and thankfully Alex believed him.

As Tony sat on the couch in the low lit living room he knew he was hiding. Not from his feelings but from the reality that there was nothing he could do about them or the upcoming wedding. There was no way to stop the inevitable. Gabby would never be his.

When someone knocked on the door he ignored it until they knocked again. He took a deep breath before he got up and reluctantly answered. He stepped back stunned when he saw Gabby. Sweet Gabby, wonderful Gabby. Beautiful Gabby standing before him as tempting as warm cinnamon rolls covered in white icing;

strawberries drizzled with chocolate. Chocolate. He'd always think of her and chocolate.

"You're supposed to be at the party," he said in a gruff tone amazed he was able to speak.

Her astute brown eyes remained fixed on his face. "You left the party early. Alex said you weren't feeling well. I was worried."

Tony gripped the door handle until he was afraid it might break in his hand. She wasn't supposed to follow him. To look for him. To look *at* him like that. He was supposed to be invisible: Alex's assistant—nothing more. Didn't she realize the danger she was in? He could kiss her right now and not regret a moment, but he wouldn't. He couldn't. He'd do the honorable thing and send her away. "You don't have to be. I'm feeling better now."

"Then come back to the party. It's not the same without you."

"Nobody will miss me."

"I'll miss you."

He lowered his head. "I can't go back."

"Why not? Is your leg hurting you?"

His whole body hurt, ached. He absently rubbed his leg. "A little. You'd better go." He turned.

She touched his arm and he spun around so quickly she cried out in alarm.

"I want you to leave," he said, afraid he'd no longer be able to stop himself and keep her safe from him. "I want you to go back to your party and your family and your fiancé and forget about me. Is that understood?"

Gabby blinked back tears. "No, I don't understand. I

thought we were friends. We used to have good times. Remember when we were tasting the food from the different catering companies and driving into town looking for paintings for the house because Alex didn't have the time? Lately I hardly know you. You've been so cold and distant. What have I done?"

He sighed as though he felt the whole world was about to crush him. She sensed his anger and he couldn't hide that. "You haven't done anything."

"Then tell me what's wrong."

He grabbed her shoulders and peered deep into her eyes. He swallowed knowing what he had to do. What he had to risk. "I've fought a lot of battles in my life. I like to think of myself as a loyal friend, but right now I'm questioning myself. For once in my life I *envy* Alex because I can't fight his youth, his looks or his money." He briefly shut his eyes. "And worst of all I cannot fight how much I love you. I want to marry you." He stepped away from her, ready to see her run. "There. Now you understand."

Gabby stared at him speechless not sure how to take what he'd said. He'd taken her breath away before but never like this. The strange fluttering in her heart became a deafening drumbeat. She couldn't tear her eyes away from him. *He loved her?* This wonderful man loved her in spite of everything? In spite of her lack of money, lack of prestige? It didn't make sense, it certainly wasn't sensible, but she didn't care.

Tony patted her on the head as though she were a little girl. "I know it sounds silly to you. I'm a lot older and—"

Gabby stopped his words with a kiss. She would show him how much of a woman she was. She gripped the collar of his shirt and kissed him as though if she stopped he'd disappear. Then she pulled away and said in a breathless rush, "I love you, too. I didn't know it until this moment." She caressed his cheek amazed by the strength of her feelings, shocked that she hadn't realized them until now. "Yes, I will marry you."

Tony stood unable to move. "Are you serious?"

Gabby grinned. "Do you want me to kiss you again?"

"No." He slid one arm around her waist like a hot spoon slipping into chocolate ice cream. *"I'll* kiss *you* this time." He crushed her soft body to his solid form, his mouth covering hers with all the passion he'd pent up for months. She moaned with pleasure as his hands skimmed her full curves with deliberate enjoyment. "I can't believe this," he said in a barely coherent grumble.

Gabby kissed his chin. "Will you take me as I am?"

"Definitely." Tony unzipped her dress and lowered her sleeves.

Gabby laughed at his eagerness and shook her head. "No, I mean would you run away with me?"

He paused. "Oh."

She drew away from him unsure of what his response meant. She wrapped her arms around herself as though suddenly chilled. She hadn't thought everything through. What if he didn't want to marry her? What if he'd just wanted a fling? Had she miscalculated? "I can't go back. I can't face all those people. Especially..." She gazed up at the ceiling blinking back tears then returned her gaze to his face. "Especially my sisters. I'm letting them down."

Tony gently cupped her face in his hands. "We don't have to do this."

Gabby turned and kissed his palm, which had felt warm and safe against her cheek. "But I want to." Her tears slowly dried with the warmth of her love as she studied him. "I want to spend the rest of my life with you."

Tony gathered her in his arms and held her tight. "That was it."

"What?"

He drew back and gazed at her with wonder. "My one wish. I lied when I told you I didn't know what it was." He pressed his lips against hers then whispered, "You've just made it come true."

perfect timing

. . .

Cassie and Drake from "Table for Two" will always have a special place in my heart.

They were the first couple to show up in print after years of trying to get traditionally published. Their road to romance was just as rocky as my road to publication (although, fortunately, not as long).

One challenging barrier was Cassie. Her insecurities threatened to end her chances of a happily ever after. Fortunately, before she lost Drake forever (his patience had run thin), she finally faced her fears and helped me launch the Henson series.

I don't always write stories in order, so this tale came to me years after they'd been married.

But the flash of a story that showed them newly married came to mind.

A change was in the air for these two and Cassie's old fears had started to rise to the surface again. What would she do?

I wrote this short story to find out.

Cassie Henson left the doctor's office in a daze.

She didn't know whether she felt thrilled, terrified or a mixture of both.

What she did know was her life was about to change.

She walked out the front glass doors of the square-shaped building, which sat on the corner of a nondescript suburban complex on the outskirts of DC, and slowly wandered towards the main road and the bus stop. She absently tugged at the collar of her coat against the chill autumn air.

What would be the best way to tell her husband the news they'd been hoping for? It had to be perfect, memorable.

Cassie stopped once she reached the sidewalk, vaguely aware of a roaring sound and the blast of wind that swept past her, snapping at her jacket and making her face tingle. She adjusted her glasses and marveled at how unseasonably warm it felt for autumn, when only moments before it had felt chilly.

It took her a moment to realize the warmth had come from the large mechanical beast that had rushed by her, with the bright smiling face of someone advertising dental work on its red and blue side, was the bus she needed to take home. She started to run but knew she wouldn't make it or be able to catch the driver's attention.

She softly swore. If she hadn't been dawdling she could be on her way home now, preparing a special surprise.

The thought made her smile.

She'd happily wait another thirty minutes for the next one.

Waiting was good. It slowed things down. At least it felt that way.

Cassie sat on the hard bus bench, her heart beating with joy and anticipation.

The doctor's visit had only confirmed what she'd suspected. Before today, she'd already taken two pregnancy tests and had scheduled a doctor's visit (third time's the charm, right?) just to make sure.

Weeks ago, after she'd gotten the first positive test result, she'd thought of calling Drake at work and telling him.

Then she thought of how busy the day might be for him and decided to wait for dinner, brushing aside the email she'd printed off from her business manager, urging her to consider a speaking tour for the reprinted edition of one of her books.

However, the test's result was too fresh in Cassie's mind for her to focus. Instead, she cooked chicken piccatta—making sure the lemon-butter sauce bathed the golden-brown cutlets in perfect balance—and was ready to set the table when Drake called and apologized, telling her to eat without him because he'd be working late.

Her heart fell as she watched a perfect moment slip from her fingers.

The next few days followed the same routine—she'd cook a special meal, he'd cancel dinner at the last moment, and she'd eat alone.

It didn't bother her. His two restaurants were doing well and he'd gotten an opportunity to expand his brand. She was proud of him.

And his busy schedule gave her pause. What if the test was wrong? Perhaps she should wait.

When Drake finally managed to have dinner with her, the following week, Cassie was so thrilled to be with him, she let the moment come and go determined that the next dinner would be extra special and the moment right. She had to make sure it was truly memorable. Not ordinary like this.

And because she was so eager to prepare for the right moment, the right dish, the right time; Cassie missed the moment right in front of her.

She didn't see the love in her husband's gentle brown eyes as he gazed at her across the dinner table. She didn't hear the tenderness in his tone as he told her how glad he was to have this time with her and apologized for being so busy. She didn't notice how carefully he answered her questions about his day and asked about hers. Later, as her mind went through the grocery list of items she needed to buy, she didn't feel the gentle brush of his fingers on her arm when he passed her in the kitchen as she washed the dishes.

Nor, at night, when she turned her back to him as she thought about which dinner plates she would set out and whether to include candles or not, did she feel the butterfly soft caress of his hand against her shoulder as he whispered goodnight, or hear his soft sigh of longing when she didn't respond.

Instead she drifted off to sleep and decided to take a

second test before making the announcement just to make sure.

The second test confirmed the first and, again, her heart was buoyant. She rushed out of the bathroom that rainy morning eager to tell Drake before he left for work…but the second she met him in the hallway, her mouth open, her eyes bright, the right moment flew away on the wings of a phone call.

Drake swore, glancing at his phone with a frown. "What is it?" he asked her.

Cassie didn't respond right away. She wasn't sure how.

He sounded impatient and looked distracted, her joy dimmed. Now wasn't the right moment. He was never abrupt with her, but her husband could look fierce when he was in a certain mood.

It didn't matter how handsome he was, with one glance he could make a robin stop mid-song. He looked fierce right now and she felt her courage falter.

"Cassie?"

He said her name, but the underlying note of irritation in his deep voice didn't help. She swallowed and met his penetrating dark gaze. "What?"

"Did you want to tell me something?"

The phone continued to ring. His gaze continued to hold her still. Her heart continued to race. But she couldn't tell him. Not yet. She sent a nervous glance towards the phone unable to hold his gaze. "Shouldn't you answer it?"

She noticed his grip tighten before he said, "It's just Eric."

She met his eyes. "It could be important. You should take it."

He hesitated and narrowed his eyes a fraction, as if he was beginning to grow suspicious. She didn't want him questioning her because the mood was all wrong and the timing terrible.

She'd tell him when he got home.

Cassie flashed a bright smile and kissed him on the cheek. "Try to talk with your brother without getting into an argument," she said before she turned and walked away.

But an argument happened anyway and Drake returned home fuming. It took a few days to settle the dispute and make sure the two brothers were on speaking terms again and not once did Cassie feel comfortable telling Drake her—their—news.

Emotionally exhausted and anxious for reassurance, Cassie convinced herself that a doctor's visit was the best action to take before she told him anything. The last thing she wanted to do was raise his hopes then see them dashed if she was wrong. She doubted people would get two false positives but she wanted to make sure.

Now she was certain. The baby they'd hoped for would be coming in about six months. They'd wanted it. It had been the first thing they'd teased each other about: Having three children. This would be the first.

Their first child together.

He'd be so happy.

Cassie looked up at the blue sky dotted with white clouds and released a happy sigh. She wouldn't wait any longer. She pulled out her phone, eager to tell him now.

"Excuse me, does this bus go to Dupont Circle?"

Cassie looked up at the middle aged man who'd asked the question. He stood beside a woman who seemed to be of similar age. They both carried bags sporting the logo of the National Air and Space Museum. She briefly wondered what adventure had led them so far out of the heart of the city.

She told them that the bus didn't go there. Then gave them instructions on the best route to take until, with some probing questions, she realized they'd be better suited to go to Metro Center instead.

By the time she said goodbye and waved them along their way, the desire to call Drake had disappeared. She didn't want to tell him the news over the phone.

In person would be much better.

She'd get a ride to his Blue Mango restaurant, where she knew he'd be today, and surprise him. She couldn't wait to see the look on his face.

***

She didn't think it would look like that.

Cassie stood across the street from the restaurant as the black Kia that had driven her there merged into traffic. She saw Drake holding the door for an attractive woman: A woman who could wear a fitted cream suit and had the waist the size of a delicate tea saucer.

And he was smiling.

Drake didn't smile easily. Cassie wasn't sure she'd

ever seen him smile like that. And he wasn't one to flirt, so how had this woman managed to get him to look at her like that? Who was she?

Cassie didn't feel jealousy.

In the past, the other woman's svelte figure would have made her feel insecure about her own full figure. But she'd gotten past that and accepted herself and Drake's love for her.

She didn't even feel resentment that the other woman managed to benefit from one of Drake's rare smiles.

She felt disappointed. After such a terrible ordeal with his brother, someone had gotten Drake to smile before she did.

The special moment had slipped away, once again.

Now, this moment, didn't seem necessary or even important.

She blinked back tears. Why did that special, perfect moment keep eluding her? Why was it proving so hard to find?

She turned and darted into a building before Drake could see her and called to get a lift home.

She could tell him at dinner.

Or perhaps tomorrow.

Yes, tomorrow sounded right.

AT HOME, as Cassie picked her way through dinner, her mind felt lost in a smoky haze. She wondered if she should ask him about the woman. She must have told him something amazing or he wouldn't have looked like that.

But then she realized Drake, with right, would then wonder how she would know about this woman and if she told him she'd seen them, he'd wonder what she was doing outside the restaurant and should she tell him the truth or lie or…?

"What's wrong?"

Cassie stiffened at her husband's tone. "Wrong?"

Drake motioned to her plate. "You're not eating."

"Oh," she pushed the red beans and rice on her plate as if spreading them around made it look like she'd made headway, the smoky feeling lingering. It wasn't only in her thoughts, she felt it surround her, but that didn't make sense. "Just lost in thought," she said. "Working on another book."

He covered her hand with his, the lyrical cadence of his island background softening his words. "It's too soon for you to start lying to me."

She blinked, surprised. They'd only been married a year. "Lying?"

"You're not working on a book."

He had her there. She usually told him about her projects. "It's not really a lie. I'm…" She sighed. "I have a few things on my mind."

"I'm all ears."

His phone rang.

She sighed. Of course the phone would ring, she knew tomorrow would be better. Or maybe she should wait for the weekend. "You can get that."

He put his phone on mute. "It can wait."

"No really, please."

He continued to stare at her.

"Drake, please," Cassie said wondering why the smoky sensation felt even stronger. "It could be important."

He picked up, never shifting his gaze from her face. "Hi," he said in a bored tone, then, "No, now's not a good time. Right." He hung up and set the phone down. "Better?"

She sniffed the air, was she really smelling smoke? "Do you smell that?"

Drake frowned. "Don't change the subject."

"I'm serious."

He blinked. "So am I."

And so was the fire alarm that burst into a loud wail.

Drake jumped up from his seat with such force he knocked the chair to the ground. He swore.

They both raced to the kitchen where he pulled out a burnt pastry and set it on the stove.

"I didn't see you put that in the oven," Cassie said.

Drake released a long sigh of regret. "It was supposed to be a surprise."

"It certainly is that." Cassie turned and opened the window, missing the flash of sadness that briefly touched his features before she turned back to him. "Was it supposed to be edible?"

He shot her a look.

It wasn't a look that could freeze a bird in mid-song, but it was one that could strike terror if you didn't know him. Since she did, she bit her lip, trying not to laugh. The awful mess and the disgust on his face amused her, but she wouldn't even giggle because she loved him too much.

Drake had little humor when it came to food. Especially wasted food since he'd grown up hungry.

Her heart always ached when she remembered his past, how he'd been a young man who'd struggled to raise his younger siblings on ketchup packets and hot water.

Her amusement quickly died. She grabbed a fork from the utensil drawer and walked over to the burnt mess. "Perhaps if we remove the blackened bits—"

He gently pushed her hand away. "No."

She playfully bumped him with her hip and leaned forward with her fork poised to strike. "Let me just see if I can—"

Drake came up behind her, trapping her in a bear hug where she couldn't move. "Apologize."

Cassie gasped in surprise. She tried to wiggle free. "Why should I apologize?"

She felt him nod towards the stove. "Because this is your fault."

"My fault?" She tried to turn to him, but he tightened his hold without hurting her.

"Yes," he growled. He lowered his voice to a whisper, his warm breath tickling her ear when he spoke. "This is what happens when you worry me."

Her heart kicked up speed. She stared at the stove glad he couldn't see her face. He suspected something, but she didn't want to talk about it now. She forced a laugh. "There's nothing to worry about."

He paused then his voice became even softer, but no less insistent, when he said, "Are you sure?"

She nodded.

He didn't release her.

"Drake, trust me. There's nothing to worry about."

She heard him sigh before his arms fell to his side and a selfish part of her wished he hadn't let go.

She thought about the fashionable woman at the restaurant, the smile she'd put on his face, and the frown he had now because she'd distracted him and ruined his surprise.

If she told him now, the memory would be tainted by the smell of smoke and the sight of a burnt disaster.

He deserved better.

She'd tell him later.

But the later she expected didn't come.

A BELOVED RESTAURANT up in flames…

Cassie absently listened to the news report as she sat on the couch and sketched out a new speech. She'd turned down the idea of a speaking tour her manager had sent her, but did have a new topic she wanted to expand on.

Drake Henson…

Her head shot up. She stared at the TV screen and saw her husband's face.

…the owner of…

Cassie grabbed the remote and turned it off. If she

didn't hear it, it didn't happen. It couldn't have happened. There had to be a mistake.

She began typing on her laptop, vaguely aware of what she was writing.

The phone rang with a noisy insistence.

She decided to ignore it.

She typed faster. Harder. She was too busy to answer it. She had work to get done.

It was probably her best friend Adriana, anyway. She didn't have time to chat.

Mercifully, the ringing stopped, bathing the room in an exquisite silence.

That lasted ten seconds.

The phone rang again, more urgently if that was possible.

It could be Adriana again or her brother-in-law, Eric.

She'd speak to them later.

Later. Later. Later. Everything would be better later.

Ring! Ring!

Ring!!!

Why did the damn phone have to keep ringing??

Silence once again followed, then ringing again. It could be her brother Clay. It could be her sister-in-law Jackie. It could be her mother.

No, not her mother. That would be worse.

Cassie continued to type, taking pleasure in the sound of the mechanical keys on her keyboard. She wouldn't answer the phone.

Let it ring. It didn't rule her. She had too much to do. She didn't want this fear to be real.

She didn't want to acknowledge the possibility that Drake wouldn't be coming home. That she'd never hear his voice again, feel his arms around her. That he…

No! No, she refused to think about it.

They'd only just begun their life together. They'd made a home, had started a family and now…

It was too soon for him to leave her and yet also too late for her to tell him so many things. He'd die never knowing about the baby.

How could she have been so foolish?

Why hadn't she told him? Why had she kept waiting for a moment that wouldn't come?

The laptop screen turned blurry from the blinding tears that she refused to let fall.

More ringing and ringing and ringing pounded against her ears.

She disconnected the phone and welcomed the silence.

But this time the silence fell like an avalanche, it didn't offer her any calm, it suffocated her under its weight. She fought to find peace. Desperately grasped at it.

She turned sharply to the front door when she heard footsteps.

Had the police come already?

They usually came to alert the family and she could imagine their faces. She imagined one young, one older; one with a husky build, the other slender. They would try to be solicitous.

But she didn't want them to come, to tell her anything—please.

Not yet.

Later.

But the footsteps stopped at the door.

She held her breath as she waited for the doorbell to ring. To hear a knock on the door and…

The doorknob slowly turned. Had someone used the spare key to check up on her because she hadn't answered the phone?

Cassie felt like jumping up and stopping them, telling them she was fine.

But it was too late.

The door swung open.

She closed her eyes. Waited for someone to say her name.

But no one did. She heard someone sigh.

"I'm fine," she wanted to say, but her closed throat, constricted by the force of unshed tears, wouldn't let any words pass.

The footsteps made their way to the couch; she felt the seat cushion sink as someone sat down beside her.

They were there to comfort her, that's why they offered no words. There was nothing to say.

She didn't sense that the person was Adriana. First, her friend wouldn't have been so silent and this was someone who weighed a lot more than Adriana did, perhaps by a hundred pounds. They smelled different too. Adriana never smelled like…spices?

An arm wrapped around her shoulders and drew her close, offering a familiar comforting embrace.

Cassie sank into its warmth, past pleasures surfacing

in her mind. She knew this embrace. These arms. How they held her was so familiar.

Too familiar.

She squeezed her eyes tight, too scared to open her eyes and possibly believe…

With the caution of a mouse treading past a sleeping cat, Cassie slowly opened one eye and saw a familiar neck, a well loved jaw line, she recognized the shape of his ear.

She opened the second eye and recognized the man's shoulders, the soft feel of his blue cotton shirt.

Drake! This was Drake. He was here!

How???

She shoved him away and stared, stunned, not sure she could trust her eyes. Was she dreaming?

Drake stared back equally shocked. When he finally managed to speak, it held a note of worry and caution. "Cassie. What's going on? One moment you look like you're going to fall apart and the next you're staring at me like I'm a ghost."

"I t-thought…" She paused, trying to taming her shaking voice. "I thought you were dead."

His brows shot up. "Why would you think I was dead?"

She gestured to the TV screen, its black screen reflecting their images back to them. "They said you were." She shook her head. "I mean, they said there was a fire then they showed your picture and said your name." She hung her head and buried her face in her hands, feeling both relieved and humiliated.

Drake pressed a feather-light kiss on her forehead

before he drew her close again. "No, no, love. The restaurant owner was someone I knew and this clever but unrelenting reporter, who'd once done a complimentary piece on one of our restaurants years ago, somehow roped me into making a statement about the tragedy. That's all." He held her tight. "It's okay."

That's probably why the phone had been ringing; people had seen Drake on TV and wanted to talk about it. The ringing had all been harmless.

If she'd answered, she wouldn't have ended up so anxious.

After a moment, Cassie said, "Why do you smell like spices?"

"Oh," Drake said surprised. "Didn't I tell you?"

She pulled back and looked at him. "About what?"

"The spice lady."

Cassie shook her head and watched in amazement as Drake's face lit up as he told her about signing a contract with a new wholesaler who was offering him a great deal.

Food. Of course the attractive woman had made him smile because she'd been talking about *food*. She should have guessed that.

"And that's my news," Drake said and then, "Now it's your turn."

"My turn?"

He hesitated. "Don't you have something to tell me?"

Cassie searched his face. Dawning slowly came. "You *know*."

Drake shook his head, his tone growing soft. "I don't know anything for sure unless you tell me."

"But you can guess," she said feeling a bit deflated. So much for hoping to surprise him.

"I want to hear you say it."

"Does it matter?"

He held her gaze, his face vulnerable, and his voice low. "Yes, to me it matters a lot."

It mattered to her too. She took a deep breath then said in a rush, "We're pregnant."

He blinked, nonplussed. "What?"

"What do you mean 'What?'"

He blinked again. "What?"

She looked at him alarmed. "Drake, you're shaking."

"That's the news?"

"Wait," Cassie said studying his face. "You mean you didn't guess?"

He released her and took a deep breath. "No." He closed his eyes and rested his head back. "I didn't suspect a thing."

"Then what did you think my news was?"

He threw an arm over his eyes and groaned.

She poked him in the side. "Drake, you have to tell me."

"I've been busy a lot lately and I thought maybe that upset you and…I saw the email from your manager on the countertop. I thought you'd decided to go on a speaking tour to give us some space or something and didn't know how to tell me."

Cassie started to giggle.

Drake shook his head. "It's not funny." He rested a hand on his chest. "If I wasn't so happy right now, I'd be annoyed." He sent her a cutting sideward glance. "You know how much this means to us. Why was it so hard to tell me?"

She swallowed, licked her lip. "It wasn't that it was hard." She licked her lip again, her reason felt ridiculous now. "I wanted the moment to be perfect. I kept trying to find the right time."

Drake studied her for a long moment before he softly said, "You're joking, right?"

Cassie laughed without humor. "No, I wish I were. Each time I wanted to tell you never seemed the right moment." Her voice began to shake as she thought of the fear that had gripped her only a few minutes ago. "And then when I saw you on the news I thought something had happened to you. And the thought that I wouldn't get a chance to tell you made me feel so stupid and guilty and shallow and vain. I realized I'd been a fool and waited too late because I wanted to wait for the right moment and then I realized there's no right moment and—"

Her husband's tender lips stopped the rest of her words in a warm velvet kiss and she surrendered as he gathered her close and held her tight. All her fears disappeared, all her shame too.

This was what pure joy felt like. It felt like a strong embrace, smelled like a touch of curry, saffron and sweet mango chutney and tasted like home.

A bright future awaited them.

But she wouldn't wait for the future; she would cherish right now-every day, every moment.

Each one was special.

Drake cupped her face then whispered against her lips, "You're wrong, you know."

Cassie stared at him confused. "Wrong?"

"Yes. You did miss the right moment to tell me. It was the perfect time."

"I did?" Her voice cracked in surprise. "When was that?"

Drake grinned, the warmth of his gaze echoing in his voice. "Anytime," he said before he kissed her once more.

sweet serendipity

. . .

This bonus story allowed me to address one of the main issues only hinted at in "This Time Forever". While the two main characters, Cat and Bryant, were different in many ways (mainly personality) they also had major physical differences that made them appear to be an odd pair.

In this short story I wanted to write about this glaring issue by having Cat face it, with the one thing that had brought them together—food.

No one went to Tanya's Café for the coffee.

It was serviceable but no more than warm brown water made bitter or sweet according to your taste. Nor did people make their way to the rectangular sized building, squeezed between a flower shop and a tax preparer for the ambience, which was less than serviceable.

The inside boasted cream colored walls, with images of coffee mugs and muffins painted by someone with more enthusiasm than skill, a few chairs and tables that looked as if they'd just been delivered from the factory (since few people used them, preferring to buy their items and leave), two tiny windows and a black and white cat that liked to hiss.

The reason people showed up at Tanya's Café, and had done so for the past fifteen years, was because of the muffins. The sweet succulent scent could lure the most avid health nut for blocks. Once inside the café, the display case housed a wealth of various temptations from banana nut, blueberry, chocolate, raisin and seasonal flavors like spiced pumpkin. They all promised the same soft, sweet, delectable experience.

But of all the things to put the café on the map was their cranberry muffins.

That was the only reason why Bryant Meadows had made his way to the small place on a drizzling autumn morning, flashed a big smile and ordered two teas (that were even less serviceable than the coffee) and two muffins.

"I'm sorry we don't have them," the cashier said in a bright tone blissfully unaware of how much she'd ruined his day.

"I'm sorry?"

She blinked impossibly long, dark lashes and said, "They weren't delivered."

"Delivered?" he repeated to make sure he'd heard correctly.

"Yeah, there was some sort of delivery issue." She

shrugged as if her action was a sufficient enough explanation. "But we got plenty of others." She motioned to the display case. "Lots of people like the chocolate ones."

He didn't look down, but his smile dropped as did his patience. "I didn't come here for chocolate—" A sharp tug on his sleeve abruptly stopped his words.

"It's okay," the woman beside him quickly said, "we can order something else. The scones look nice."

Bryant bristled at the thought, his English sensibilities coming to the forefront, although he'd left the country of his birth more than twenty years ago. He wouldn't trust this café to make a proper scone if they were threatened by gallons of kerosene and a lighter, but he was too polite to say so.

"Or the banana muffins," she added as if reading his mind.

He took a deep breath, letting Cat's words assuage some of his temper. He'd wanted to treat her to something better but he wouldn't make a fuss. "Fine," he reluctantly agreed. "Two."

The cashier beamed. "Your daughter has good taste."

Bryant sent the cashier a look that could have withered a rose. "She's not my daughter," he quietly said.

The cashier's mouth fell open then closed then opened again as she searched for words.

"Two teas and two banana muffins," he repeated slowly in the same quiet tone, since the cashier appeared to have lost the ability to not only speak but move.

She nodded an apology before she hurried to fill his

order. In her rush, spilling the tea, leaving a soggy mess of paper towels in her wake, and grabbing the wrong muffins before Cat corrected her.

Cat Kayode watched the cashier in pity.

No one did well when Bryant's mood shifted. He'd entered the café all smiles, that's what he did well. He handed out smiles with the ease of a dandelion spreading seeds, but he wasn't smiling now. And when Bryant didn't smile he made people nervous.

And that beautiful smile of his had disappeared because the cashier had referred to Cat as his daughter when in truth she was his girlfriend.

There were rare moments, like this, when Cat wished she didn't look nearly a decade younger than her actual age. That she looked at least in her mid-twenties (she was nearly thirty) instead of someone just out of high school. Bryant was only eight years older, but moments like this made the age gap feel greater and highlighted other differences too.

Bryant silently found a table for them near one of the small windows and sat. He took a muffin and handed one to her.

His good mood hadn't returned and she didn't know how to get him out of the funk he was in. Was he embarrassed? They hadn't gone out frequently as a couple and she knew that they made an odd pair. Did that bother him? Should she make a joke of it? Ignore it? Did it bother him that he looked that much older than her?

It would have been more of a coup if she'd been good looking. Men liked to flaunt getting younger women, but she didn't rate high in that category. Too plain. That didn't bother her but she didn't want it highlighted either.

Cat looked down at her clothes, perhaps next time she'd dress up a bit more so she'd appear more mature, if that was even possible. Nothing about her screamed 'girlfriend of a successful business owner.'

She inwardly laughed at the thought. She'd never imagined herself dating someone like Bryant Meadows. Tormenting him? Yes. Teasing him? Absolutely. She'd done so for years because he'd proven an amusing target with his easy people pleasing ways, polite, over considerate demeanor and good looks. Not that there was much to say about his looks except that they were compelling—dark skin, dark eyes, close cropped black hair. With his tall build he should have appeared intimidating—which he could be but rarely was, he was too charming for that.

Cat had pictured herself with someone more edgy. Perhaps someone with one or two tattoos in the shape of a viper or hawk; a nipple piercing or even an earring or three; maybe even a large skull shaped onyx ring. But Bryant didn't wear any jewelry at all, and although he was a graphic designer, he looked as artistically inclined as a forensic accountant in his dark trousers and dark purple sweater. But perhaps that was because he was also someone who negotiated contracts which he did for the company he owned with his best friend Keeden.

THE MUFFIN SAT UNTOUCHED. Bryant didn't pick at it or even shift it on the plate. She knew he wouldn't waste it. Perhaps he'd give it to his father later.

"It's not half bad," Cat said, nearly finished with her own, hoping to encourage him to try it.

He sent her a glance, doubtful. "You like it?"

She nodded.

He pushed the plate towards her. "Then you can have mine."

"But—"

He shook his head. "It's okay. I'll get something else later."

He turned away and lifted his tea but didn't drink it. The steam that had once wafted from it had already faded. It wasn't like him to brood. Had what the cashier said really affected him that much?

Cat sipped her tea uncertain.

She was still getting used to moments like this. Moments others would consider banal and ordinary but were rife with minefields for her, because Cat didn't do things in ordinary ways.

For one, she didn't socialize. Especially not in cafés. She wouldn't be here if Bryant hadn't invited her. She was used to being on the move: working for her parents, cooking for an event, cleaning, trying to avert disasters in the delicate balance of her household. Not sitting in front of a handsome man eating muffins. That was the second extraordinary wrinkle. The man.

Handsome or not Cat didn't have much experience with men and relationships and, truthfully, hadn't had much interest. Give her a horror movie or a pro wrestling match any day. But this particular man enjoyed cooking and food as much as she did and she liked being with him, even though he put her in awkward positions like this.

She had grown used to being with him when it was just the two of them in his kitchen or living room, but out in public she didn't know how to act. They still hadn't told anyone they were an official couple yet. Plus she couldn't do 'couple' behavior, not that he expected her to, but the cashier's words had thrown in her face what had truly bothered her.

She was used to being invisible.

Being with Bryant made her anything but that, it was as if in his presence a spotlight suddenly shone on her and she didn't know how to cope.

She also didn't know how to comfort. Was Bryant hurt by the cashier's words? Angry? Annoyed?

It didn't help that he wasn't eating and continued to hold his tea as if he were posing for a cologne ad or something.

She pushed the muffin back towards him. "Try a tiny bite."

His gaze met hers—cold and hard before they quickly shifted towards the exit. "No."

She was used to that look. She'd met it before.

Before their feelings for each other had changed,

Bryant would try to avoid her (at best) but when he didn't manage to (at worst) he'd send her that villainous look, which had always let Cat know his disdain for her.

She hadn't thought he'd ever look at her like that again.

She thought about apologizing, but didn't think she had anything to apologize for. "Okay, then—"

"I want to leave." His words were clipped, formal but insistent.

Cat nodded and placed the untouched muffin in the brown bag ready to go.

THE SOGGY AUTUMN sky no longer sent down spits of rain but sat above them in a staid grim assortment of grey clouds.

Bryant's mood hadn't improved. She thought of annoying him, as a way of distraction, since that was something she always managed to do best.

She took his hand, expecting him to pull away, but he surprised her by wrapping his fingers around hers and she heard him release a sigh.

The warm feel of his hand felt nice.

That was one mystery solved. He wasn't angry at her. But he was still upset. She glanced at his profile, but it told her very little.

They walked a few blocks in silence and she wasn't sure where they were headed and didn't care to ask. She spotted a garbage can and thought of something. "I once saw this movie where a woman found a decapitated—"

Bryant squeezed her hand in gentle warning. "Shut up."

"It's not as gross as it sounds and there's a point where—"

"I don't care."

Fair enough. She knew how much he hated gory things. It was the wrong way to try to distract him.

"Bryant, what's—"

He abruptly stopped in front of the brightly lit window of a convenience store and let her hand go.

Cat inwardly flinched, surprised by how cold and bereft she felt.

An ordinary moment that felt so much more.

She followed him inside. Keeping her distance. That was it. Be like a shadow, if she wasn't close no one would notice her. No one would make a mistake about them. Perhaps she could make a habit of it in public. Perhaps…

"Cat."

She turned sharply to him. Saw him several yards away in the frozen aisle section.

"I've asked you twice if you want this."

She noticed the pint of chocolate chip ice cream he held up. She could readily imagine dipping a spoon and enjoying the smooth, creamy vanilla-flavored ice cream with chunks of chocolate. Did he really have to ask her?

"Oh, sure."

He placed the pint in his basket and lifted another.

"Surprisingly, there's also salted caramel." He took a step towards her. "What do you think?"

Salty and sweet and delicious? Was he trying to torment her? "That's nice too." She took two steps back, glancing at the next aisle, which was clear of anyone. "Get whatever you want."

"I know what I want," Bryant said, continuing to close the distance between them. "I'm asking you what you want."

Cat waved her hands, hoping he'd stop walking towards her and head to the cashier. "Anything. I'm not picky. You know that."

He frowned. "Why do you keep moving away?"

She glanced around. No one was looking and if she moved fast…

She dashed over to him and said in a low voice, "Let's get both and once we get to your place I'll heat up a portion of the banana muffin and then serve it with the salted caramel ice cream. I think you're going to be impressed. How does that sound?"

He sent her a long considering look. She saw a flash of disappointment enter his brown gaze before he nodded and said, "Fine," then went to the counter.

What was that look for?

Once they left the store she didn't reach for his hand again and he didn't seem to notice. He was too lost in thought.

He also looked sad.

She opened her mouth wishing she knew what to say, and closed it again knowing she didn't.

No more avoiding it. As much as she hated dealing

with emotions, something was bothering him and she'd face the issue.

SHE'D JUST CLOSED the car door when she finally gathered up the courage. She touched Bryant's hand before he started his jeep. At least they were alone now. She felt safer here with just the two of them.

"I'm sorry the cashier upset you," she said, "but it was a simple mistake. It's because she couldn't believe we'd be together."

"What?"

"That's why she thought I was your daughter," Cat clarified since Bryant was looking at her confused. "That's what's been bugging you, right?"

He sagged against the seat. "I'm sorry."

"It's okay." She never imagined he'd be so sensitive about it.

"I told you about this place and then I couldn't deliver. I know you're upset."

"Upset?"

"The banana muffin isn't as remarkable as the cranberry and you keep going on about it because you don't want to make me feel bad. But you don't have to pretend that it's that good."

"I wasn't pretending. It's really nice."

His jaw twitched. "I didn't come all this way for *nice*. But I'll make it up to you."

Wait. Why were they talking about muffins? Had she missed something?

Cat cleared her throat. "Bryant. The cashier upset you, right?"

"Yes." His jaw twitched.

"Because—"

"Because she lied to me."

Cat shook her head. Now she was the one confused. "What?"

"I don't know why she lied. But she did. You could smell the muffins, couldn't you?"

The entire café smelled of muffins. "Yes, of course, but—"

"Do you know why?" Bryant didn't give her a chance to answer. "Because the muffins are made on the premises, they aren't delivered. I know this because I asked the owner about them a couple weeks back."

"Then why did she say there was a delivery issue?"

He pounded the steering wheel. "Exactly! Why did she lie? She could have said they'd run out or something. But they were there. I know they were. They keep some extra in the back even though the display case didn't have any. That's also something else I found out when I spoke to Melissa." She remembered seeing the cashier's name tag, but the way he said her name had a familiarity that put her on alert. He didn't sound as if he'd just learned it today.

"You've been there before?"

"Yes, many times."

"And you talked to Melissa?"

"Yes. She promised me. She said if I came in, anytime, she'd make sure to have one for me."

Cat briefly closed her eyes in understanding. "I bet she expected you to come here alone."

"Why would I come alone?"

She playfully punched him. "You idiot."

"What?"

"You always act unaware when someone is interested." She'd seen him ignore her sister's former crush on him for years.

He shrugged. "I didn't say I was single."

"What smile did you give her?"

"Smile?"

"Yes."

"My regular one and then we were talking about food—"

"That did it. She was half in love with you. Your smiles are lethal but then when you add them to your passion for food they are purely seductive."

He looked embarrassed. "No, it's not."

"I've seen you get extra discounts at the World Foods." She'd even spotted the fishmonger give him extra ounces of halibut when he thought no one was looking. Bryant knew how to charm even when he didn't mean to.

But he looked unsettled.

"I may have been a bit over enthusiastic," he finally admitted. "And she may have gotten the wrong end of the stick."

"So no cranberry muffins as punishment," Cat concluded.

He swore.

She patted him on the back. "Never mind. I'm glad

that's why you're upset and not because…" She let her voice fall away and stared out the window.

"Not because what?"

She felt embarrassed to admit it.

He poked her in the arm and when she turned to him he sent her a knowing look. "You thought I was worried about the age reference?"

She nodded.

He shrugged. "Doesn't bother me that you look young." He playfully pinched her cheek. "Demons tend to age at a slower pace."

She swatted his hand away and laughed in relief, used to his teasing. In the past he had avoided her as if she were a dark shadow from the underworld.

Then a thought struck her. It was a little devious, but it could work. "Wait here."

A FEW MINUTES LATER, Bryant stared at her curious as she slid into the passenger seat carrying a bulging brown paper bag. Soon the interior of the jeep was enveloped in a sweet aroma of sugar and cinnamon.

"What's this?" he asked when she set the bag on his lap.

She opened it and pretended to waft the scent towards him.

"Cranberry muffins," he said in awe. He turned to her. He didn't smile, he had a habit of not smiling at her, but he looked happy. "How did you get them?"

"Well, we can't go back there of course."

He narrowed his eyes, suspicious. "What did you do?"

"Don't get mad."

"What. Did. You. Do?" he repeated slowly.

She winked. "I told her I was your niece."

For a second Bryant stared at her stunned and Cat braced herself for his reaction.

But she didn't expect a kiss.

A sweet, warm, delicious kiss that reminded her that for all their differences they made a perfect pair.

catnip dreams

. . .

I like telling stories from different viewpoints.

But, truthfully, I never imagined I'd tell a story from the viewpoint of an animal. Especially a cat (I didn't think they cared).

But Alfonso from "Dream of Me" had opinions.

Lots of opinions about his live-in Jarrell and the steps he should take to be happy. I found his ideas amusing so I let him tell his story.

THE LIVE-IN WAS IN BAD SHAPE.

He had a lot of names—Honey, Babe, Son, Jarell—just to name a few, but I'm not big on names so never really thought of him in those terms.

To me he was the kind-hearted servant who didn't laugh anymore. And I was worried about him. I don't like worrying.

But his scent was all wrong, like a parched land

desperate for rain: Full of dry cracks and crevices hungry for the tiniest drop. Desperation seeped from every pore of his skin. He was desperate for something I couldn't give him. Something no one seemed to. He had shelter and food so that wasn't the problem.

But he never slept. Not once. He barely napped. He hadn't always been this way.

It was eerie.

I'd been hopeful that night would be different. The days leading up to that night had felt different. He checked his reflection in the glass, which he rarely did anymore. His steps sounded a bit better, lighter, his scent less gloomy (like wet socks left out in the rain) and more cheery (like warm socks fresh from the dryer or that had fallen into dew soaked grass). He even gave me more treats, not crickets unfortunately. I miss crickets, the other place used to have lots of them, but not here. This place was clean, very clean, the live-in had someone come in weekly and make sure. They even got rid of the smallest sign of cobwebs…no spiders for me either…sigh.

So that night there was no crickets, no cobwebs and no hum of the machine in the living room nor the clacking of keys.

Instead the live-in sat on the couch, the night air different than any time before, and held the cell phone tight in his hand as if he were afraid it would fly away. (I know the feeling. I'd once had a big juicy grasshopper in my grasp and lost it. It hurts to this day).

He tapped the cell phone in a strange pattern, waited, swallowed, then he spoke and his voice was deeper, sweeter than usual. He'd used that voice with me once. When we'd first met and he'd lightly touched my paw. It was a very soothing voice. He didn't use that voice often, made me a little jealous that he was using it with someone else.

Must be someone special. I noticed his pulse had picked up speed as well.

He didn't talk much, but that wasn't unusual. He wasn't much of a talker. However, the way he listened was.

His breathing, usually shallow and quick, slowed. His scent changed, as if clouds had opened up and a downpour had filled every crack of the dry land.

Instantly, I was no longer jealous. I was thankful. The live-in had received peace.

He briefly covered his face with his hand, released a soft sigh. A happy sigh as if he'd been gifted a fresh can of tuna.

Then he nodded.

His breathing slowed even more.

Then he fell asleep.

Fast asleep.

I know. I know I told you he didn't sleep. But he did that night. I was startled too when it happened. Couldn't believe it.

Because he didn't sleep before.

He paced, he sat in his large chair, near the black humming machine, and watched a screen for hours, mumbling to himself while wearing strange earmuffs. He likes making noises on the keyboard, sometimes hitting one key lots of time, but when I tried, he got mad.

I mean is there ever a good reason to shout like that? I know I've got one eye, but I've still got two ears.

He apologized soon after—a quick cuddle in his arms, kiss on the head and a belly rub, the guy knows how to please—but he can be very territorial. Sometimes he reminded me of a stray I'd once met in my old life. She'd found her way under the wooden fence that surrounded the garden patch. She'd managed to flatten her body as thin as a leaf then popped out again full size once she reached the other side. She'd had hard edges, like she'd found herself on the wrong patch once too many times and gotten the swipe of claws or nip of teeth.

Like her, the live-in remained tense, guarded, most times. He was kind to me, don't get me wrong. I liked how he smelled, how when he returned home he'd call out to me (I wasn't always called Alfonso but that's another story) and have me purring within seconds, but in spite of that, he remained distant, distracted. As if his body was present but his mind was elsewhere.

I knew life on the outside was hard. I heard the stories. When the live-in came home from being on the outside, he always looked as if he'd met an unfriendly feral with friends. A cat I used to know lost an ear that way, another nearly lost their life. I lost an eye 'cause of its dangers. I wasn't naïve. I knew how lucky I was.

The live-in didn't seem to. Even though he had food, shelter and me, like the stray, he was up at night. Always busy. He did a lot of things. He'd cook, he'd clean, rearrange his books.

But he did not sleep.

Until now.

I hadn't been certain at first. During the phone call he'd become slumped over in a strange way and then slowly fell down to his side. His breathing even and smooth.

I walked up to the cell phone, but I didn't touch it. I'd once knocked it off a table—the temptation had been too great. There it sat staring at me and the edge of the table was soooo close…it just took two light taps and then it clattered to the floor, bouncing on its edges before it settled on the wooden ground. He hadn't been happy about that either, but hadn't shouted as he had with the keyboard.

So that night I nudged the cell phone with my nose and shared my thanks. I heard a voice talking without pause and I tried again but knew they wouldn't understand. They rarely understood no matter how clear I am. They paused then said something but they didn't sound happy.

There was nothing more I could do so I curled up beside the live-in and went to sleep too.

HE SAT up with the speed of a startled squirrel. Instantly alert. He stared around the room—doubly brightened by the sun that clashed with lamplights. Then he picked up the cell phone. It had fallen to the ground—not my fault. I waited ready to be blamed, but he didn't look at me. He held the cell phone as if he'd never seen it before. As if he didn't know what it was.

Then…it was strange…a look of horror crossed his face.

Horror like discovering someone else had pissed in your litter box.

He swore. He rose to his feet then fell back down as if his legs no longer worked. "I fell asleep."

You'd think that was a good thing. I am a master of sleep. I know sleep. This live-in needed sleep.

He got a good night of it.

He should be happy.

But he wasn't. He sounded miserable.

Someone hadn't just pissed in his litter box they'd pooped in it too and not covered it up. His hand shook. "I fell asleep," he said again his voice barely a whisper, agony in each word. "God how long was I out?" He groaned, rubbed his face. "This is bad." He swore. Squeezed his eyes shut. "What should I do?"

I offered a suggestion. Told him he should sleep a little more. But he stared ahead as if I hadn't made a sound. I wasn't surprised.

Live-ins never listen.

***

THAT NIGHT STARTED A NEW ROUTINE. He had a bunch of other phone calls that ended the same. There'd be the giddy scent of excitement. His breathing would change. He'd sit on the couch, he'd listen. Peace descended and he'd fall asleep then wake up miserable.

Every. Single. Time.

Then the calls stopped. He started pacing again. He sat in his chair and tapped on the keys with his earmuffs on but didn't seem happy.

He stopped sleeping again.

I started worrying again. This live-in was good to me. I didn't want to lose him.

And I might have if they hadn't come: the attendants.

There were two of them. One had quick, light footsteps like a chickadee walking across a sheet of ice.

The other hesitated. She kept freezing in place. It was weird. She reminded me of this cat that had never been on grass before. They'd reach out a paw touch the surface then snatch it back again. Took him forever to get used to the sensation. The attendant had the same uneasiness, maybe she'd never seen such polished wood floors before and was only used to carpets like the worn ones at my old place.

I'll be fair, I tolerate attendants. I'm not a big fan of being fawned over—getting washed, brushed, nails clipped and the like—but I'll endure. I frighten most attendants so they're quick. But these two were different.

The live-in seemed to sense it too. His mood slowly changed.

The scared one smelled nice. Like soap, nothing fancy or floral, just clean and fresh. When she stroked me she did so with a steady hand. Although she was frightened (I could smell her fear) she wasn't afraid of me. I couldn't help myself, I licked her hand. I was so thankful I didn't intimidate her (and I liked her so much) I wanted her to come back again.

But even more it was her affect on the live-in. He changed. His breathing was different, calmer; similar to the way it had been during those strange phone calls. He was tense, but in a different way, more focused, anticipatory. Like having a chipmunk in your sight calmly eating away, its back to you and it doesn't know you're there. It's a powerful feeling knowing that you could strike at any moment but you won't because you just like observing their innocence, their lack of awareness.

He was like that. He a cat; she a chipmunk.

The two attendants didn't notice him watching them.

I did.

I noticed how he kept a studied distance. How he folded his arms or rested them on his hips. And his voice again. I noticed the tender tone of his voice. I think he sensed the frightened one's fear and wanted to help her.

Her cell phone rang and she went into the kitchen. Ran really. Something must have spooked her.

The live-in grew tense again. The kind of tense that worried me.

The attendant with footsteps like a chickadee and a scent like strawberry-kiwi jam couldn't keep his interest. He kept glancing towards the kitchen before he excused himself and left.

The remaining attendant was lovely but worried, saying strange things like, "I don't know what's gotten into her. I hope she can hold up. I wonder if I shouldn't have asked her to come here with me."

I was glad the other attendant had come and didn't understand what the problem was. Sure the other attendant was a little skittish but so what? She was nice. I liked her, the live-in liked her. I told the remaining attendant that but she just smiled at me.

The same indulgent pretty smile as the other one. The one that used to spend the night—many nights—but didn't anymore. The one who smelled like roses. She used to pat me on the head. Three quick pats—one, two, three. As if I were a little dog she expected to bark. It was insulting. I don't like to be patted. Especially on the head.

But then she'd offer me a treat and I'd forgive her. She admitted to the live-in that she wasn't used to cats.

The voices from the kitchen carried. I heard the words but couldn't quite make out their meaning. I knew he was calling her a name she didn't like. He sounded amused; she annoyed.

The conversation didn't really matter to me. It was what happened next.

After the attendants left the live-in clapped his hands and laughed.

A full blown laugh.

Then he lifted me up and he held me close as he spun around in a circle. I felt his heart racing. "I'd thought I'd lost her. Now I get to see her again."

I didn't know what he meant, didn't care really. I just let him continue to hold me, glad he was happy. I hadn't seen him that happy in a long time. No, I don't think I'd ever seen him that happy, except once when he was in his special chair in front of the screens. There was this one moment when he acted as if he'd gotten the best spot on the couch—you know the spot, the one that's soft but has a solid center? It was that kind of joy.

He had that now.

He didn't sleep that night either.

But for the first time that felt okay

HE WAS READY TO MATE. It was clear the night he brought her home.

The scent of dry, parched land had been replaced with something muskier—ripe, earthy, potent. He'd never smelled like that when he was with Roses. His scent had been different, more subdued, but not this time. There was nothing subdued about it. His body reeked of sweat, longing, primal urges. I barely remember those feelings anymore (one day I woke up sore and groggy and never had those feelings again) but I can still smell them in others.

He had it bad.

For his sake I didn't want her to leave. He called her Candice, but like I said, I'm not big on names.

To me she was the live-in's catnip. He was a little wild because of her: smiling for no reason, laughing, sad then happy then sad again. But she didn't know her power over him. She was still skittish.

You have to be careful with skittish ones. You never know how they'll act. I didn't understand why she thought she had to go. Roses always used to spend the night, although she didn't anymore. But this one didn't understand.

When Catnip followed him into the bedroom I made space for her on the bed but she didn't notice. She just sat stiffly in the chair beside the bed like I'd seen one attendant do when the live-in and I had gone to the vet. There was a thick ankled woman with a big dog that kept shaking. Never did find out what was wrong with him, not that I asked.

But this one sat the same way as that woman, cautious. The tantalizing scent of a female in heat clung to her skin. I knew it was tempting him. But she was holding back. It didn't make sense.

She wanted to. He was willing. Well, he had been before she talked him to sleep. Don't know how she managed that, but she did.

She got up and left.

I went after her.

She closed the door.

I told her that was wrong and she was quick to listen and opened the door again. I offered her one of my favorite possessions. She decided to play with me and I did a little performance and got her to stay a little longer, but not long enough. Not even a little warning growl did much to sway her.

I couldn't get her to stay.

I felt bad about that.

HE'S AWAKE.

I'm looking up at him. He's still in bed.

It's morning but he doesn't open his eyes. I always know when he's not asleep. He sometimes thinks he can trick me by staying still but it doesn't work.

This time I sense he's not trying to pretend, but he doesn't want to get up either. He sweeps his arm over the empty space beside him—Did he think she'd be there? Did he want her to be?—before he opens his eyes and looks at the empty chair.

He stares at it as if it had turned into a clear bowl filled with fat bellied goldfish swimming round and round—so close yet so far out of reach. No matter how much you pressed your paw against the glass you can't get them. He has that look. He smells sad. I hate when he's sad and he's sad a lot.

So I talk to him and he looks at me. He reaches down and softly scratches me under the chin, I'm purring in spite of myself.

He sighs and looks at the chair again and says, "What am I doing? I'm an idiot to hope she'd…"

He doesn't finish but I agree with him. He is an idiot because he should be happy he got to sleep again, even if she's not there, but it's not enough.

SHE'S HERE AGAIN. The heat is so strong it fills the room. They want it. They want each other.

They're sitting on the couch and he's wrapping her

paw. They're talking. So much talking and no wait… they're heading for the bedroom.

This is it.

It's going to finally happen. He's getting in bed and…

Nooooo

She's sitting in the chair again. What is wrong with this woman? What's wrong with him? Is he worried he'll scare her away?

Can't he smell the heat on her? Can't she sense how much he wants her? It wouldn't take much. They want it so bad.

She talks to him.

He falls asleep.

I sigh.

She'll never spend the night.

I was wrong. Catnip did spend the night just not the way I thought she would.

Not in the comfortable bed, which would have made sense since Roses did all the time, but instead she slept in the big black chair.

That was a dangerous choice. Not even *I* sleep there. That was his territory. The live-in was very possessive.

When he woke up I tried to warn and tell him what he'd find, but he just yawned and smiled and told me I'd get my food soon.

Who cares about food!! He was going to get angry

and shout again and then Catnip would never come back.

I tried to talk to him again.

He didn't listen. Why don't they listen????

Then he went into the living room and froze when he saw her.

I froze too. I waited to smell the scent of anger, but…no it was relief. Joy.

And a primal mating scent mingled with a different kind of possessiveness as he studied her.

I don't drool, but I'd seen a cat drool every time it smelled chicken.

The live-in had that same look now.

I expected him to lick his lips and pounce, but he crept up to her instead.

I thought he was going to grab her, but he knelt down and smiled up at her as she slept in his favorite chair.

He beamed.

I'd never seen that expression before. He got a blanket—one that still smelled like the old attendant who'd given it to him, like cocoa beans and vanilla, and covered her with it. He reached to touch her face before he stopped himself.

He sighed and it sounded happy and sad. Why was he still so sad?

I jumped onto her lap. It was a very comfortable lap. She was a very comfortable person.

I knew he was in a good mood because his footsteps were different. I knew it was because of her. I hoped she'd soon become a live-in. He didn't eat breakfast often. Especially not scrambled eggs and plantain.

Catnip woke up slowly. Then all at once. I jumped down.

She barely paid attention to me. She quickly folded the blanket.

She tried to leave. I considered swiping her ankles to get her to stay but he called out to her and stopped her from leaving.

They ate together: their scent, their breathing, their movements in sync.

Then they left together while the sun was fresh in the sky and by the time he returned the sun had long disappeared but he was the happiest he'd been in a long while.

He sat on the couch and covered his face. I jumped up beside him and nudged him with my head.

I got the affection and attention I wanted but even more I got a wistful grin before he mumbled, "She still doesn't know how much I..." He didn't finish but mumbled something about three days.

He barely slept that night. That was no surprise, but this time I wasn't as worried about him. This sleepless night was different.

This sleepless night he didn't pace, or cook or sigh.

This sleepless night he smiled.

And somehow I knew one day his sleepless nights would be over.

Because he'd finally found what he needed.

He'd found her.

the perfect christmas

. . .

Jessie and Kenneth have a complicated history. Getting them together in "The Sapphire Pendant" was no small feat, but I managed to do it and felt accomplished.

Then the stones showed up.

I don't know why they did. I had no intention of writing a short story featuring Jessie and Kenneth.

But then the stones showed up.

And I knew there was a story because I had to know why and what they meant. Jessie read stones. Were they meant for her or did they mean something else?

I had to write and find out and, in the process, uncovered a story that surprised me.

HE DIDN'T LIKE THE SIGHT OF THE STONES. ALTHOUGH they looked innocent as they lay on the front doorstep, glittering under the cold rays of a winter sun, they reminded him of something, but he couldn't remember what, that left him with a feeling of dread.

"What are those?"

Kenneth Preston turned to his wife, Jessie, as she came up behind him carrying two bags in each hand, her red winter hat tipped at an angle. They'd been holiday shopping for their adopted daughter, Syrah. It was to be their first Christmas together as a family and they were both eager to make it special. He didn't want anything to ruin it. Somehow he felt the stones would do that.

"Probably nothing," he said, bending down to remove the stones.

She grabbed his arm. "Wait. Don't touch them."

"Jasmine, don't—" he said calling her by her given name. Only he was allowed to call her that.

She stepped closer, putting her two bags in one hand, and gazed down at the stones. "Just give me a minute."

He didn't want to. He didn't like the look of interest in her gaze. The stones were bad news, he could feel it.

Kenneth put the keys in the lock and opened the front door. "Come on, it's cold."

"I wonder who left them here. The arrangement is very peculiar." She bent closer to examine them.

His wife had a special gift and affinity with stones. He respected that, but not now. He wanted her for Syrah and himself. He didn't want to share her attention with anyone. Especially someone who'd left a strange puzzle on their doorstep. A puzzle that reminded him of something, but he didn't know what. "Jasmine, we need to put the bags away before Ace gets home," he said, using Syrah's nickname.

She scooped up the stones in her gloved hand and offered him a bright smile. "Coming, coming." She brushed past him into the welcoming warmth of their house, the scent of sugar and ginger greeting them. But as he closed the door behind her, he felt as if the cold chill of winter had followed them inside.

———

"WHAT ARE you going to do with the stones?" Kenneth asked Jessie later that evening as they prepared for bed. He didn't really want to know, but couldn't help his curiosity.

She slipped under the bed sheets and rested against the headboard. "Nothing. I don't know who they're from or why they were left."

He swallowed, hoping she was telling him the truth. Was it a warning? Had the scandal about his past created still more consequences for them to face? He felt a fissure of unease, like a tiny, hair-thin crack in a piece of glass. A crack of a memory wanting to emerge from the corner of his mind where he'd safely kept his past sealed. But he fought it; he wanted to stay in the present. They'd come through so much. He didn't want anything to separate them again. "Are you sure?"

"Am I sure of what?"

"That you don't know anything?"

Jessie held his gaze, a quick flash of fire lighting them. "You think I'm lying?"

Kenneth lowered his gaze and swallowed. He didn't want to argue. He didn't want to upset her because he was afraid. Afraid of… He inwardly groaned. He didn't know what. But something ugly gripped him, something frightening and troubling. He didn't want anything to destroy the perfect Christmas he planned for them. Nothing could go wrong. He wouldn't let it. The memory teetering on the edge of his mind would stay there. He smiled, bent forward and kissed her. "No, I wouldn't dare. I—I just don't like the look of them."

"They're nothing to worry about."

He nodded and slipped in beside her, taking deep breaths. He had to believe her. Although he didn't like the stones, he had to trust her. He couldn't think she knew something and wasn't telling him. He couldn't think that maybe she was protecting him. He had to believe that there weren't secrets between them. That was the past. They were now joined together for life. He'd need two thousand lifetimes to show her how much he loved her. This Christmas would be the start of many—nothing could go wrong. Unless…

"What's the matter?" Jessie said in sharp tone.

"What?"

"You stopped breathing."

Kenneth froze. "I did?"

"Yes. Why? You always do that when you're upset."

He avoided her gaze. "I was just thinking about something."

"What?"

He shook his head. "Nothing." He gripped his hand into a fist. He was already lying to her and he didn't want to, but felt that he must. Trust meant not asking questions, and he couldn't doubt her.

"I won't do anything without telling you first," she said as if reading his mind.

He took a deep breath. "I know." He kissed her again, assuring her as much as himself. "Promise me anyway," he whispered against her lips.

She smiled. "Promise."

He felt some of his tension ease, then turned off the lamp light, but the darkness that settled around them seemed to find its way inside him too.

AND THAT DARKNESS still followed him a week later. He didn't know why the stones bothered him or why he felt suddenly restless. He stared at his reflection in the full-length closet mirror, straightening his tie one morning as he prepared for work, almost not recognizing the man staring back at him. Only a couple of weeks earlier he'd been so happy about the upcoming holiday and now he was filled with dread.

He left the large closet and walked into the bedroom, then felt someone grab his arm and pin it behind him. "Tell me what's bothering you," a female voice whispered in his ear.

Kenneth couldn't help a smile as his pulse quickened; he could overpower his wife in one swift move, but he'd let her believe she was in control, for now. "Should something be bothering me?"

She tightened her hold. "You tell me. You haven't been yourself the last few days."

"Nothing's wrong."

"Want to arm wrestle?"

He slipped out of her grasp, swung her over his shoulder and pinned her to the ground. He gazed down at her with a smug grin. "Want to lose?"

He waited to see her temper flare. Watched to see her beautiful brown gaze turn hot. She'd probably make him late for work and he'd enjoy every minute of it. But instead of her typical heated look, he saw worry tinge her eyes.

"I feel you pulling away from me," she said.

He didn't move, the truth of her words holding him still. She was right. He could feel it himself and didn't know why. They were now married, she was his new wife and he loved their life together and yet something gnawed at him and seemed to grow the closer Christmas came. His fears seemed foolish and there was still so much yet to know about each other, but there were still things he didn't want her to know.

Because he had no words, he kissed her, lingering over the sweet taste of her mouth, hoping it would be enough to remove the worry from her eyes. He wanted her to think about the tall pine they'd decorated that stood in their living room, the colored lights that covered the house, and the apple cider they'd had by the fire. The holidays were supposed to be happy, especially this one. He'd keep whatever darkness that hovered, within him. He drew away from her and smiled. "How can I be pulling away, when I'm right here?"

Her gaze searched his, the worry deepened. "Kenneth, what's wrong?"

His pulse quickened again, this time from fear instead of desire. Why did she have to know him so well? "I can't stop thinking about the stones," he said, releasing her.

Jessie sat up. "I think I may know who the stones belong to. One of the clients at the store may have left them because he heard about me and—"

"I don't want you to have anything to do with him." He didn't mean to sound harsh, but something told him it was important that she stay away.

He waited for her to argue. Waited for her to tell him that he was her husband and not her jailor and that she'd do what she wanted to do.

Instead, she nodded. "Okay."

"What?"

"I said okay. If it bothers you that much, I'll leave them, but…"

"But what?"

"I sense that whoever left the stones seems to want protection and help. They're not dangerous and—"

Kenneth shook his head. "I don't care. Stay away."

"Fine. I will." Jessie lightly touched his cheek, her fingers warm and soft against his skin. "Is that all that's bothering you?"

God, he hoped so. He took a deep breath and stood. "I'd better get going." He lifted her to her feet, resisting the urge to hold her close in case he wouldn't let her go.

THERE WAS TOO MUCH SNOW. It wouldn't stop. It was two days to Christmas and it seemed people would get the white Christmas they hoped for. But to Kenneth, the continuous snowfall chilled him. It didn't fall with a soft light touch, but seemed to pound the earth, suffocating everything around him in white.

"Dad, are you okay?"

The sound of his daughter's voice caused him both pleasure and pain, reminding him of what they'd both gained and lost. But he couldn't think about his brother, Eddie, right now. Nothing else mattered except making Syrah happy and helping her forget her brutal past. He turned from the window and looked at her as she stood there, wearing an oversized sweater he'd wanted to donate but she'd decided to keep. Their dog, Dion, stood by her side. Kenneth forced a smile. "Of course I am."

She bit her lip. "I'm not."

He forced his smile not to waver. "Why not?"

She sent a nervous glance towards the window. "They were supposed to work, but I'm not sure they will."

"What are you talking about?"

She shook her head. "Nothing."

"What's wrong?"

She looked at him. "Mom's not home yet."

He checked his watch. He'd assumed she was upstairs. Jessie was usually home before him. "I'm sure she'll be here soon."

He couldn't let Syrah sense his unease. He knew she was looking forward to their first Christmas as a family, and was used to being disappointed. Did she have the same fear he did? That happiness may be out of reach for them? They both loved Jessie, but they also both knew that the ones they loved could hurt them the most. He knelt in front of Syrah, keeping his smile in place and his tone light as he pressed down his own concerns. "I bet she had to finish up her holiday shopping and lost track of time."

Syrah nodded. "Yes, it's going to be all right, right?"

He tweaked her chin. "Right."

But an hour later, Kenneth wasn't so sure.

"I'm sure it's nothing," Jessie's eldest sister, Michelle, said when he called her. Her tone was practical and no-nonsense, reflecting the businesswoman she was. "She's a walking accident. If you worry about her, you'll grow old fast—trust me. Just wait for her to come home. If anything's happened, you'll know."

When he called Jessie's other sister, Teresa, the advice was the same but said in a lighter more soothing way. She was a woman who believed in visions and herbs and that reflected in her words. "Your years together have only just begun, your paths are inter-twined and you're bound together unless you break them."

He gripped the phone. That didn't make any sense. "Just let me know if you hear from her."

"I will, but you have to trust her."

"Of course I trust her."

"With everything?"

He briefly shut his eyes. Teresa was sweet, but strange and he hadn't called for marriage advice. "Yes."

"Good, then she'll be fine. You both will."

But when another hour passed, he didn't feel fine. And his worry grew. He called her cousins and then anyone else he could think of, but no one could reach her. He had to believe that nothing was wrong. That she hadn't defied him and seen the man she'd mentioned about the stones against his wishes.

He had to believe that she was okay, even when another hour passed and he saw a story on the news about a woman's body being found near the bay.

"Poor woman," Freda, his housekeeper said, passing by the family room to head to the kitchen.

It couldn't be Jessie. She was just somewhere where her phone didn't work and the snow…

Kenneth looked out the window, his hard gaze sweeping over the snow blanketing the ground and weighing the trees with its oppressive white hand. It looked harmless, but it could be so many things. Why did he hate snow so much? He felt an answer to that question as the hair-thin crack of memory tried to expand in his mind, but he violently silenced it with his will.

In two days they'd have their first Christmas as a family. A Christmas to help him forget the pain of his past. He had the right to be happy, to fight for his joy and his place in the world.

As a child, he remembered one winter clearing the driveway for Jessie's family, the Cliftons. Eddie had promised to do it—and taken the advanced payment Mr. Clifton had given him—but did only half the job.

Kenneth had finished it up, hoping nobody would notice. He made sure there was not a flake left.

"You mustn't try so hard," Mr. Clifton had told him with a glint in his eye.

He didn't understand him at first and felt a little hurt and defensive. He was embarrassed that he'd gotten caught and angered by the criticism.

"You'll wear yourself out for no reason." He now knew what Jessie's father had meant. That he didn't have to try so hard to please, to be accepted, but it was still a lesson he was learning. He wanted this Christmas to be one of the best Jessie and Syrah had ever had.

Three hours later, he paced. He couldn't report Jessie missing. Not yet. Not ever, he corrected. Because she would be home soon. She had to be.

Another hour passed. He felt himself falling apart. He grabbed his keys, determined to find her, then stopped when he heard the front door open.

He met her at the door. "Where have you been? We've been waiting for hours. Do you know how worried Ace was?" he said. "I had to lie to her to get her to eat dinner then lie to her again to get her to go to sleep. Do you know how many people I called? You couldn't let anyone know where you've been, what you were up to? What happened?"

Jessie blinked, then sighed with regret. "I hardly understood a word you said. But I know you're upset and I'm sorry. Now take a deep breath and speak slowly and in English."

It took Kenneth a moment to realize he'd spoken in

French. The language of his youth, the language of his heart. He could feel himself shaking as his anger and fear mingled within his veins. He hadn't shouted at her like that before and always tried to be careful to control his temper. He knew the danger of losing control. He took her advice and took a deep breath. As he exhaled, he felt his shield of anger slip away, as if a filter had been removed from his eyes, and he finally saw his wife clearly.

He saw the cut on her lip and the bruise on her cheek and his heart twisted. He rushed towards her, then stopped himself from touching her. "What happened?"

Jessie pressed her hands together as if in prayer. "Don't be angry."

Kenneth folded his arms. "I'm already angry, what did you do?"

"This older woman was getting mugged—"

His arms fell to his sides. "You went after a mugger?"

"She said her life was in that purse and I couldn't just stand around and do nothing." Jessie held up her hand before he spoke. "I know he could have had a knife or a gun, but he didn't. Unfortunately, he got away and she was so shaken that she asked me to go with her to the police and I did. I'm sorry, I didn't even think to call you. And then on my way home, a car swerved and hit me. Not too bad, so don't worry, and then my phone died and it was just chaos. But I left the hospital because I wanted to come home."

His voice cracked in surprise. "You were at the hospital?"

"The woman who hit me was insistent I get checked

by a doctor, so I just did it to calm her. I'm so sorry I didn't get in touch with you somehow. It was just a crazy day and—"

Kenneth spun away and headed upstairs.

Jessie followed him. "You're not going to forgive me?"

He headed for their bedroom. "I'm glad you're home."

"But you're still angry," she said, staying close behind.

He kept walking.

"Kenneth."

"Keep your voice down."

"Why? Syrah's probably already awake after your shouting rampage. At least she knows I'm home."

"It wasn't a rampage."

"It came close and I don't know why—"

"A woman was found dead today," he cut in, his voice raw with emotion, "and I thought it was you."

"Why would you think that?"

"I don't know!" And he truly didn't. He didn't understand his lingering anger. She was safe, but his heart still hammered in his ears.

"Why are you shouting at me again?"

"I'm not shouting."

"It's my fault!" another voice said. They both turned and saw Syrah standing at the end of the hallway. Her voice broke. "It's all my fault."

Jessie shook her head and walked towards her. "Honey, no it's not. We're just—"

She took a step back before Jessie could reach her. "I

had Freda leave the stones on the doorstep, but they didn't work."

"What are you talking about?" Jessie asked.

"I know I don't have your gift with stones, but when Aunt Teresa told me that they were special stones that could bring good luck and protection to a house, I thought…" Her words fell away. "I was wrong."

"That's why they had that feeling," Jessie mumbled to herself. "I'd wondered about that." She knelt in front of Syrah. "You weren't wrong. And you didn't do anything bad. But why would you think we'd need that? What are you frightened of?"

Kenneth came up behind Jessie and cupped Syrah's chin before she could reply. "You're safe now."

Jessie hugged her. "You don't need to be afraid. We're a family now and we're happy." Jessie turned and looked up at Kenneth. "Right?"

He looked at Jessie then shifted his gaze to Syrah, a chill coursing through him. He knew what he had to say, even though he didn't mean it. "Yes." He kissed her on the forehead. "Now go back to bed or I'll take one of your presents away."

Syrah wrapped her arms around Jessie's neck and hugged her. "I'm so glad you're home."

Jessie hugged her back. "Me too."

"KENNETH, I SAID I'M SORRY," Jessie said, closing the door behind them once they were alone in their bedroom.

"I know." He sat on the side of the bed and faced the window. "It's fine."

"It's not fine if you won't even look at me."

He rested his head in his hands suddenly feeling tired and not knowing why.

"I don't understand…" Her voice died away and he heard her footsteps retreat. "Okay, I'll leave you alone. I'll sleep with Syrah tonight then and—"

He reached her before she could get to the door. He swung her into the circle of his arms and held her tenderly. "I'm sorry," he whispered into her hair. "I didn't mean to shout and I'm glad you're home safe."

"Your heart's pounding."

"Hmm."

She looked up at him. "Kenneth?"

He heard a world of questions in her voice, but he wasn't ready for them yet. He held her tighter and said in a teasing tone, "Why won't you leave your husband and be with me? Your husband's an idiot sometimes."

Jessie tapped his chest with her forefinger. "I won't leave my husband because I love him too much. And he needs me."

Kenneth lifted a brow in surprise. "He needs you?"

"Yes, so he can stop pretending." She drew away from him. "What's wrong? And don't act like you don't know what I'm saying. You're free now, you don't have to pretend anymore, remember?"

"I want Christmas to be perfect."

"Christmas will be wonderful, okay? What's with you and Syrah recently?" she asked. "You don't have to be Mr. Perfect anymore. We've got our schedule planned from Christmas to New Years' with family and friends. Even if things go wrong it won't matter because it will be one of many memories we'll get to share. I don't know why she thought we needed the protection of those stones."

ON CHRISTMAS EVE, they sat in front of the fireplace, the tree lit and the remnants of the sugar cookies and eggnog they'd enjoyed set to the side. Jessie told him and Syrah tales of when she and her sisters would wait up for Father Christmas. She made Syrah laugh and Kenneth watched them, wondering why he still felt so tired instead of happy. It was Christmas Eve.

Stop pretending, Jessie had told him. You must trust her with everything, Teresa had said. And she was right. Jessie was the one person he could be real with.

He needed to be honest. He hadn't really been afraid of her ignoring him regarding the stones, or getting killed. Those fears gave him a shield against what truly scared him, that the Christmas he was hoping for would be out of reach.

He worried that he wouldn't feel as he was supposed to. He'd never found Christmas a magical season. He'd never had a chance to believe in Father Christmas. All his life, he'd smiled his way through the season to please others, but he always felt like a fraud because the presents and the lights never warmed his heart. And he knew the truth would disappoint her. But pretending had become too much of a burden.

He kissed Syrah goodnight before she went off to bed, then Kenneth sat alone with Jessie on the couch.

He realized that he hoped by making Syrah and Jessie happy, and that their joy would somehow stir something in him. That he'd feel what the season was about. He didn't want to tell her that every song left him feeling numb and he felt exhausted under the weight of a cheer he didn't feel. "I've never liked Christmas. I always lie and say I do, but…"

She looped her fingers through his and he gained strength in her touch. "Go on."

"When I first saw those stones, I didn't know why they bothered me so much, but then I remembered one Christmas when my father got drunk and smashed the ornaments on our tree. I don't know how old I was but I remember how they sparkled even as they shattered and scattered on the ground." He briefly shut his eyes. "I can't feel Christmas. The importance of it…. I can't…I can't feel it. I know I'm supposed to be ecstatic."

"You don't have to be."

"And there's this memory that keeps trying to come back."

"Why won't you let it?"

He rested his head back. "Because I don't want to."

"Maybe you need to."

He turned to her, his eyes clinging to hers. "Most of my memories hurt."

"I know." She patted her lap. "And you don't have to fight them alone anymore, you have me."

A smile softened his mouth. "Are you inviting me to sit on your lap like a good little boy?"

She frowned. "No, I was offering you a place to rest your head." She began to stand. "But if you're not interested—"

He pulled her down. "You know I am," he said in a deep voice.

Kenneth took a deep breath and laid his head down, letting himself surrender to the memory that had been haunting him, trying to become fully formed in his mind. He drifted to sleep, remembering another Christmas blanketed in white.

White was everywhere. White like snow, except he saw the white of a doctor's lab coat, the nurse's shoes, the hospital walls and floors. There were paintings of cartoon characters in the halls, but he didn't recognize most of them because he didn't get to watch TV much. He remembered a white pillow and a metal bed and the sound of holiday music floating from somewhere. And he remembered making a wish…

A wish he'd forgotten about.

He opened his eyes and although it was still dark, the darkness that had seized his soul was gone. He felt his numbness fade and it hurt, but he welcomed the pain because at least he could feel, and the anger and restlessness had gone. He sat up and looked around the room in renewed wonder. He saw the brilliant lights on the tree, the red flashing flames of the fire, but most of all, he saw a home. His home. The one he shared with his daughter who was safe in her room. The one he shared with his wife who'd fight his battles with him.

For the first time in years, he let himself remember the wish of a little boy, spending the holidays in the hospital after a beating, and his wish for a new family that loved him no matter what.

Stop pretending.

He didn't have to pretend anymore.

"Kenneth, are you okay?" Jessie asked him.

He turned to her, the fire glow caressing her brown skin. "Yes," he said, the truth of his words filling him with joy. "Yes," he said again, then stood pulling her up with him. He walked to the window and looked outside at the white snow as it lay under the gaze of the moonlight. He no longer hated the sight. Instead, he saw a whole new beginning.

As they stood by the window, he told her about his memory. His voice was soft as he spoke, his arms wrapped around her waist. She didn't speak, just listened as she rested her back against his chest.

When he was through, he took a deep breath. "You're right," he said. "It will be a wonderful Christmas."

Every Christmas before had been a disappointment to him, but not this one. This one would be like no other. One he'd remember for the rest of his life. Not because it was perfect, but because his long ago wish had finally come true.

bonus

Turn the page for some fun!

Second Helpings Word Scramble
Instructions: Unscramble each word using the clues from the stories.

1. HISW ENO → _ _ _ _ _ _ _ _

Clue: *What Tony wanted to give Gabby*

2. NGITIM → _ _ _ _ _ _ _

Clue: *What Cassie was waiting for to be perfect*

3. TEWES → _ _ _ _ _

Clue: *How Cat described the serendipity*

4. TPINCA → _ _ _ _ _ _ _

Clue: *What Jarrell was to Candice, according to Alfonso*

5. SAMRTISCH → _ _ _ _ _ _ _ _ _ _

Clue: *Kenneth's childhood wish was for a family at this holiday*

6. ETALOCOHC → _ _ _ _ _ _ _ _ _ _

Clue: *Sweet treat that paired perfectly with wine*

7. FINFUM → _ _ _ _ _ _ _

Clue: *Bryant's favorite cranberry treat*

8. YAMILF → _ _ _ _ _ _ _

Clue: *What Kenneth always wanted*

9. MEOH → _ _ _ _ _

Clue: *Where the heart is*

10. TRAEH → _ _ _ _ _ _

Clue: *Where love lives*

11. YOJ → _ _ _

Clue: *What love brings*

12. ELOV → _ _ _ _ _

Clue: *What all these stories celebrate*

Answer Key

1. ONE WISH
2. TIMING
3. SWEET
4. CATNIP
5. CHRISTMAS
6. CHOCOLATE
7. MUFFIN
8. FAMILY
9. HOME
10. HEART
11. JOY
12. LOVE

about the author

Dara Girard, an award-winning, national bestselling author of more than fifty novels and many short stories, from romance to suspense, loves telling stories.

Born in the US to immigrant parents, Dara enjoys pulling from her Jamaican, British, Nigerian heritage and exposure to various cultures to bring what reviewers and fans call "vivid emotional stories" to life. She is best known for her popular Henson Series, the mysterious Clifton Sisters, and the fun Black Stockings Society.

Visit her website to sign up for her newsletter and get sneak peeks, monthly updates on new releases, and special offers.

For more information visit
www.daragirard.com